H. Arnold Thomas

The Way of Life

H. Arnold Thomas

The Way of Life

ISBN/EAN: 9783741133183

Manufactured in Europe, USA, Canada, Australia, Japa

Cover: Foto ©Andreas Hilbeck / pixelio.de

Manufactured and distributed by brebook publishing software
(www.brebook.com)

H. Arnold Thomas

The Way of Life

THE WAY OF LIFE

.

By H. Arnold Thomas, M.A.

LONDON: JAMES CLARKE & CO.
13 & 14, Fleet Street.   1899.

First Edition, April, 1899.

Contents.

THE WAY OF LIFE.

The First Step.

" Now He commandeth men that they should
all everywhere repent."—ACTS XVII. 30.

IT was said by John Wesley of his
own preaching that he never failed
to " lay a deep foundation of
repentance." In adopting that
course he was certainly not depart-
ing from Apostolic practice, or
from the practice of Jesus Himself. When Jesus began His
ministry, the spirit of repentance
was, so to speak, in the air. There
had been a great religious revival.
John the Baptist had roused the
whole country by the prophetic
fervour of his preaching. The

1

people had come to him in crowds,
from Jerusalem and Judæa, and
from beyond Jordan, and had been
baptized with the baptism which
was "of repentance, unto remission of sins." And when Jesus
began to preach, He took up that
same strain which had made the
flinty rocks of the wilderness re-
echo. "When John was delivered
up," we read, "He came into
Galilee, preaching the Gospel of
the Kingdom, and saying, The
time is fulfilled, and the Kingdom
of God is at hand ; repent ye, and
believe the Gospel." That was His
first word.

And He gave instructions to
His disciples that they should
begin where He had begun.
Repentance and remission of sins
was to be preached in His name
to all nations, beginning at
Jerusalem. This was the message

that the Apostles were to deliver.
And they did deliver it, with all
faithfulness. When the people
were pricked to their hearts on
the day of Pentecost, and said to
Peter and the rest of the Apostles,
"Brethren, what shall we do?"
Peter was in no doubt as to the
reply to be made. "Repent ye,"
he says, "and be baptized every
one in the name of Jesus." And
to the clever and lively Athenians
St. Paul has the same word to say.
"Now," he tells them, "is God
commanding all men everywhere
to repent."

That was always the first thing
to be thought of, the first thing to
be insisted on, the first thing to be
done. Wesley had good authority
for seeking to lay deep the foundation of repentance.

You might not think it to be
the most promising method of

gathering adherents, to make a
universal demand of this sort, and
it is not the method which has
always been adopted by those who
have been anxious to bring men to
discipleship. Sometimes, indeed,
very little has been heard of repentance in Christian teaching.
Much has been said, and said with
great beauty and tenderness, of
the Divine mercy, of God's readi-
ness to forgive those who seek
His forgiveness, of the charm of
Christ's character, of the joy of
belonging to Him and being engaged in His work, of the nobility
of the Christian life, and of the
hope of immortality which the
Christian believer is permitted to
cherish. Much has been said on
these points, and not too much;
but men have not been made to
understand that the first thing to
be done is to repent. They have

been invited, in the most affectionate way, to receive Christ, to enter into His rest, to admit Him to their hearts, to follow in His steps; but they have not been told of this indispensable condition. Perhaps it has been felt that there was a better chance of gaining attention and awakening interest if the need of repentance were kept, for a time, somewhat in the background; that it might be discouraging and alarming to say much about it in the first instance. That may have been the idea. But the policy of the Apostles has received ample justification in the general history of the Church, and, indeed, there is no other possible policy. It is good to talk of the Kingdom of Heaven; but there is no Kingdom of Heaven for those who will not repent. No entrance is to be found into that

land of peace but through this
narrow gateway. You cannot sin
against God and live in His love
at the same time. The sin must
be given up, and it is best that
this should be made quite clear.

Well, do you say, that is no
doubt perfectly true, and is an
important thing to remember, so
far as bad people are concerned.
Of course, all bad people must repent, or they cannot be saved.
That should be obvious to every
one. Ah! but who are the bad
people? What is it to be bad?
That seems to be a simple question
enough. But is it so simple?
Perhaps not. Perhaps we shall
find that the rough and ready distinction that we are able to make
between good and bad is not one
that will bear very careful examin-
ation. The Pharisees had no
doubt who the bad people were.

They could lay their hands on
them, they thought, without
difficulty. They knew them at a
glance. They could classify and
label them without any misgivings.
The extortioners, the unjust men,
the adulterers, the publicans ; these
were the bad people. These were
the people who needed to repent.
That was the opinion of the
Pharisees. And it was, I suppose,
the prevailing opinion of the day.
It was, probably, an opinion that
was shared in by the extortioners,
and adulterers, and publicans
themselves. They knew that they
were the bad people. They did
not deny it, or doubt it. And
they were willing to accept the
Pharisees at their own valuation,
as models of excellence. But was
the popular view a correct view ?
Was there nothing bad about the
Pharisees ? Was it only the

publicans and the harlots who
needed to repent? There was One,
at least, who did not think so.
Christ did not think so. And it
may be, and such possibilities are
always worth a little consideration,
it may be, that Christ is not able
to think so well of us who appear
to be so correct, in all matters of
morality and religion, as we are
able to think of ourselves.

Here is one, for instance, whom
no one speaks of as a bad man.
He never yet committed a crime,
or was seriously tempted to
commit a crime. In his behaviour there always appears
to be a perfect propriety. Is
he a thief? It is a shame to
suggest such a thing. Does he
drink? You must not ask such a
question. Is he a profane person?
By no means. He does nothing
that is disreputable. He is a

decent, orderly, well-conducted
citizen. Yes! But he is selfish
to his very heart's core. Do what
you will you cannot make him feel
for any but himself. Tell him of
the sorrows of the poor. What
does he care for the sorrows of the
poor? Speak to him of wrongs
and cruelties inflicted on little
children, of wholesale massacres of
unoffending Christian populations.
You make no impression upon
him. It is not his affair. Nothing
really touches him but considera-
tions of his own prosperity and
comfort. Let his table be well
served; let his income be main-
tained; let all things go smoothly
and pleasantly with himself, or
with those who belong to his own
household, and who are a part of
his larger self, and it is enough.
He does not choose to be troubled
with the needs and miseries of

other people. Is there nothing
bad in that? Is that man a good
man who needs no repentance?
Is he not in a state of damnation,
if ever any soul was in such a
state? He is not like the drunk-
ard, reeling to his miserable home,
or the harlot who plies her shameful trade in the street. But is he
so much better than these unmis-
takable sinners?

Or here, again, is one of whom
it is said that he is living a blameless life. But what is meant is
that he is living a blameless life
before the world. And that is not
the only life that a man lives.
There is another, which may be
blameless or otherwise. It is the
life within, the life of his intimate
thoughts, purposes, desires, motives,
And what shall be said of this
blameless person in respect of that
inward life? The fruit which you

pluck from the tree has a most promising appearance. But open it, and you see that within there is little but rottenness. And you throw it away. It is bad, you say. And bad it is in spite of appearances. So also may a man look all that is fair; he may have all the aspect of a saint, and may use the language of a saint. And yet he may be a very sepulchre for hidden corruption. We think, do we, that we know what we mean by bad people. But are not those people whose minds give only too ready hospitality to every kind of shameful and filthy imagination, who are full within of meanness, of lust, of pride, of hate, though they are so fair-spoken and scrupulous in their outward behaviour, are not these also bad people? Or the indolent, the easy-going, who do not think them-

selves to be selfish, and are often
agreeable enough in their way, but
who are too lazy or too timid to
take any part with those more
energetic and heroic souls who are
battling against the tyrannies and
wickednesses in the world! Is
there nothing bad in that sloth,
that cowardice, which permits a
man thus to hide his talent in the
earth?

Or, once more, here are those
who are declining to have anything to do with religion. It is
not that they do not believe in the
great facts of religion. They are
not sceptics. They have no intel-
lectual difficulties. They do believe, in a fashion. But religion is
a thing in which they will not
take any interest. They have
other things to think of which
have a stronger attraction for
them. Their neighbours are reli-

gious, and it is good. They have
nothing to say against it—every
man to his fancy—but as for themselves, their tastes and inclinations
run in another direction. Religion
is not in their line. And is there
nothing at all blameworthy, nothing that can be called bad, in
such conduct? They are good
men, honourable men, conscientious, with a keen sense of duty.
But is not religion, then, a duty?
Is that a good son who has no
feeling for his own home; no
concern for his own father and
mother, though they have been
the best of parents to him; no
interest in the things that to them
are of the highest importance?
Is there nothing discreditable,
nothing at all shameful, in the
conduct of such a son? Very
well; but what are we to say,
then, of the man who has never

doubted that God is his Father,
or that Jesus Christ died for his
redemption, or that the Holy
Spirit has ever been pleading with
him, but who has been persistently
despising and rejecting all this
love and care, who has put it all
on one side, and scarcely given it
a thought, as though it were not
worth the attention of so clever,
or so busy a person? Can a man
be good, in the deepest sense, and
yet so contemptuous of religion?
Perhaps, after all, there may be
more people who need to repent
than we have supposed.

And why is it, if there be this
need of repentance, that it does
not take place? Why do not men
repent? One great difficulty,
perhaps the chief difficulty, is
that they do not know what their
true condition is. They have
never realised what it is they are

doing, and what it is they are
losing. They have never come to
themselves. We need to have the
truth about our own lives brought
home to us before we can repent.

And how is the knowledge of
the truth thus brought home to
us? In various ways. Sometimes
it is discovery, exposure, which
enables a man to understand what
kind of a person he is. He is
living a bad life, and is not at all
ashamed of it. There is nothing
which seems to him to be very
much amiss. He is so busy with
his schemes that he never gives a
thought to himself. It does not
occur to him to ask what it is that
he is doing. If there is now and
then a suspicion that something
may be wrong, the suspicion is
discouraged, and is easily for-
gotten. But some day he is found
out, and then, for the first time,

he finds himself out. He sees
himself, as it were, from the outside, and is able to judge of himself
as though he were judging of some
other person. His sin is no longer
a private matter, kept hidden
away in a secret chamber which
he will not himself enter. It has
become a public thing. It is
dragged out into the light. There
it is, standing out in all its nakedness, and repulsiveness, for every
one to see, and for himself to see
with the rest. When David's sin
was disentangled from his own
personality and thrown upon the
canvas, so that he could see it, as
it were, in a picture, he knew as
he had never known before how
abominably mean and cruel he
had been. It is a salutary thing,
sometimes, to get an experience
like that, bitter and humbling
though the experience may be. It

is astonishing how we can cheat
our own consciences in regard to
all the evil that is known only to
ourselves. But when the thing
gets abroad the conscience can no
longer be cheated. The web of
sophistries is broken, and we
cannot help ourselves. We see
things as they are, with impar-
tiality, with detachment. And so
exposure may be a great gain, as
involving self-revelation and leading to repentance.

But there is another way in
which the self-knowledge may
come. It may come simply from
reflection, from thinking on one's
ways, and asking oneself what
those ways are, and whether they
are good ways or bad ways. It
is said of Peter, in reference to his
act of betrayal, that when he
" thought thereon he wept." Until
he began to think of what he had

been doing, there had seemed to
be no occasion for weeping. All
his care had been for his own
safety. But when he had leisure
to think, then those bitter tears
began to roll down his cheeks, and
he hurried out into the dark,
shamestricken and most miserable.
Now may there not be many
things that we find ourselves capable of doing, that we would scorn
to do if we did but "think thereon"? But we refuse to think, or
the idea does not come into our
minds. We think about what we
shall eat, and what we shall drink,
and what we shall put on. We
think of what other people may be
saying of us. We sit and muse,
and live over again, in memory,
departed days. We wonder what
the future will be, and make plans
as to what we should do or say, if
this or that were to happen. And

we turn our attention to many
public matters. We give our
minds to politics, to literature, to
science, to the affairs of the city.
Our brains are not idle by any
means. In a sense, we may be
said to think a good deal, too,
about ourselves. We have regard
to our own interests, our personal
safety, our reputation. But one
question we forget to ask. We
will not come face to face with
our own souls, and ask honestly,
and with a determination not to be
put off, how the soul is faring.
It is, perhaps, the fatigue, the
strain of the effort that we shrink
from. For there is a consider-
able effort involved in this self-
scrutiny. Or we are afraid. No
doubt that often explains the
anxiety that men have to keep at a
distance from themselves. When
Dr. Johnson was at a place of

amusement he said that " it went
to his heart to consider that there
was not one in all that brilliant
circle that was not afraid to go
home and think." Is there some
explanation suggested there of
our restlessness, our discomfort,
unless we are at work, unless we
have some scheme to keep our
mind employed, unless we are
being amused? Oh, the cowards
that we are! And what folly
there is in such cowardice! For
we cannot always escape from ourselves. The truth must come out
at last. Some day all other things
that claim and absorb our attention will fall away, and we
shall be left alone—alone with our
own hearts, with our history
stretching out behind us, incapable
of being hidden any more, with
the meaning of it plain enough,
both as regards its general drift

and its pitiful details. And if
there is to come such a day of
revelation, is it not better now,
when some kind of amendment
may be possible, to tear away the
coverings which hide our souls
from ourselves, that we may see
what that buried life is which
flows on for ever, below all the
fret and excitement, the striving
and the toiling of our busy days,
and by the direction of which our
character is being shaped, and our
destiny determined? If we could
be sure that some Nathan would
come and reveal us to ourselves,
there would not be so great need of
this self-inquiry. But the proba-
bility is that nothing of the sort
will happen. For, in the first
place, no one knows all the truth
about us, or anything, it may be,
about our worst sins. There is no
mortal man who can lay his hand

upon them. And next, if there
were any prophet who knew all
the dark secrets of our inner life,
he might easily be wanting in the
courage necessary to hold them up
before our eyes. And so each man
must play the part of prophet to
himself. The advice of Socrates
to drunkards was that they should
look at themselves in a mirror, that
they might see what they were
like when under the power of
drink; and I remember read-
ing in the newspaper of some
woman, who hit upon the
strange device of getting a photo-
graph taken of her husband when
he was in a state of stupor, that he
might know, when he became sober
again, what appearance he had
presented. And I think it might
be useful to many if in some way
they could thus see themselves from
the outside. Should not we find

something in ourselves to be re-
pented of if we were to take such
a course? Should we find no
habit, no practices, no feelings,
purposes, motives, nothing that
needed to be got rid of? Perhaps not. Who can say? But
I can conceive that if we could
see things just as they are, if we
could look ourselves through and
through, as though we were not
ourselves, but some other people
whom we were judging, we should
then know that there was nothing
in the world of so great importance
to us as that we should repent.
"I thought on my ways," says the
Psalmist, "and turned my feet
unto Thy testimonies." Some one
has justly said that those words re-
present the turning-point of many
a man's character and destiny.
Yes, if we would but think on our
ways, in the light of the law of

Christ, in the light of the countenance of God, in the light of the Cross, of the Judgment-seat, of the great White Throne, it might well be that God would give us the grace of repentance, and that so we should take the first step in the way of everlasting life.

Saved by His Life.

"If while we were enemies we were reconciled to God through the death of His Son, much more, being reconciled, shall we be saved by His life."—ROMANS v. 10.

"REPENT" is the first word of the Gospel, and repentance the first thing that is necessary if we would walk in the Way of Life.

But now suppose that this first word has been listened to, and this first necessary step has been taken. We have come at last to ourselves, and the result of the self-discovery has been to fill us with sorrow and shame, and to lead us to true repentance. Our life in the past has been, we see, but a poor business. It has been a mistake throughout. But now we have come to the beginning of

better things. We are going to
turn over a new leaf, and to become
new creatures. That is our hope
and our determination. And
we set to work without delay to
carry our good purposes into practice.

And what happens next? Men
talk of repenting sometimes as if
it were a very simple matter indeed. You are sorry for your sins,
and give them up. You seek forgiveness, and obtain it. And all
is well. The whole thing is
plain enough. That is the impression that seems to be on some
minds.

And this is what, perhaps, we
actually feel when we are just
making the fresh start. We think
nothing of difficulties. Sin has
become odious to us. We have
lost all taste for it. We cannot
think how it could ever have had

any attraction for us. It is done
with, thank God. We have cast it
off for ever. The burden has
rolled away, and there is a delight-
ful sense of relief. We are cured
of a malignant disease, the very
recollection of which makes us
shudder. And the holy life which
is opening before us appears to be
full of charm and beauty. How
blessed it will be to walk in that
narrow way, with such friends
and companions as will be ours !
What a happiness it will be to live
honestly and cleanly, in the spirit
of prayer, supported by the Christian hope as true children of the
morning! We are eager to be
moving. The end of the journey
seems not to be very far away.
Already our feet are among the
flowers of Immanuel's land. Already we think we can discern,
though it may be through a mist

of happy tears, the glory of the
pearly gate.

But if these are our anticipa-
tions at the outset, how soon are
they disappointed! The strong
emotion that has possessed us may
carry us forward a little distance,
but soon it becomes apparent that
the way of life is beset with difficulties. Learning to be good seems
to be like acquiring an art. You
see a man painting a landscape
or performing on some musical
instrument, and you think that it
looks perfectly easy. Surely any
man could do what that man is
doing with so little sense of effort.
You could do it yourself. And
you try. But what a humbling
experience it is. What a bungler
you prove yourself to be. This is
wrong, and that is wrong. Everything seems to be wrong. And
you acknowledge that your first

attempt has come to very little. And so it is with holy living. When you begin to put your good resolutions into practice, alas! what faltering there is, what misadventure, what chagrin! You cannot do the things you would. Something within you seems to hinder your progress in some unaccountable fashion, and what was to have been so fair and perfect turns out to be a grotesque failure, a miserable break-down, and before very long you find yourself floundering in some Slough of Despond, and you are ready to say that it could never have been meant that you should be good, and that you may as well give the whole thing up without further struggle.

Now, if anything like that should be our experience, I do not know that we can do better than

make a study of that great passage
in the Epistle to the Romans, in
the fifth chapter, in which St.
Paul has so much to say about
the Christian life, and the means
by which its difficulties may be
overcome and its blessedness
realised. Anybody who will read
this passage at all carefully will
be at no loss to understand what
it is on which the Apostle is
setting his heart, and how he gets
the assurance that the desire of
his heart will be fulfilled.

He begins by speaking of Justification. "Being justified by
faith," he says, "let us have
peace with God through our Lord
Jesus Christ." By being justified,
he means being brought into peace-
able and happy relations with
God. He does not mean being
made holy in respect of personal
character, certainly not being

made perfectly holy. I know that the attempt has been made to show that there is no real difference between Justification and Sanctification. But I cannot think that they meant quite the same thing to St. Paul, though no doubt he felt them to be intimately related. A man is justified, in his sense, when, though he may have many faults and infirmities and be very far indeed from being perfectly good and holy, he is yet accepted by God as His child and His friend. And he is thus accepted whenever he is willing to join himself in faith and love to Jesus Christ, his doing that being the pledge that the desire of his heart is to be made like Christ in all things, however he may fail here and there, and whatever corruption and impurity may be still clinging to him.

But is it enough for a man to
be on such terms with God, to be
accepted, and to know that he is
accepted, and to be wishing that he
was a perfectly good man? It was
certainly not enough for St. Paul;
on the contrary, what comes out
with singular emphasis in this
chapter is his longing to be not safe
merely in the sense of being accepted, but holy, through and
through, righteous in all his ways
and all his works. See how he
proceeds : "And let us rejoice in
hope of the glory of God." And
what do you think he means by
that hope? What is this " glory
of God"? Not so much, I think,
any great vision which he is to
see, or outward splendour with
which he is to be invested. Is it
not rather the glory of being
Godlike of which he is chiefly
thinking, the glory of being made

perfect in character? All St. Paul's personal ambitions lay in this direction; and he was prepared to endure any troubles, to fight any battles, to make any sacrifices if only that ambition could be gratified. Nothing mattered if he were permitted to reach that glorious goal, to gain that heavenly prize. So much does he covet this perfected salvation that he can rejoice even in those tribulations which he sees may be instrumental in bringing about the great consummation. Anything that will "turn to his salvation"—to use a phrase which he employs in writing to the Philippians, where he is speaking in the same strain—anything that will tend to make him more Christlike, though it may be in itself a bitter and humiliating experience he is able to rejoice in.

All the most painful discipline of
life may be cheerfully endured,
may be welcomed with a solemn
gladness, if the end of it is the
realisation of that "hope of the
glory of God."

And now, what is the ground
for such a hope ?   The answer is
not far to seek.   It is just the love
of God.   If you are sure of any
man's love you will know that he
will do for you the very best that
he can.   And so Paul felt that if
God truly loved him, He would see
to it that he was made at last
perfect in holiness.   And how
does he get the assurance of this
Divine love ?   In two ways : first,
he speaks of it as a gift, or as an
effect of the Holy Ghost.   " The
love of God hath been shed abroad
in our hearts through the Holy
Ghost which was given unto us."
We are made to know and to feel

by the operation of a Divine influence that is at work within us that that love is a great fact. It is an inward conviction that we get, not by reasoning, but rather as an inspiration. The wonderful thought comes home to us as a reality, and we are sure that it is God by His Spirit, Who is thus making us aware of this most blessed of all truths. But it is not only through the quickening and enlightening influence of the Holy Spirit that Paul becomes assured of the love of God. It is in part, also, a matter of inference, of proof; for there is a great historic fact which, to the Apostle, is a sure evidence of its reality. That fact is the death of Jesus Christ. " God commendeth His own love towards us, in that, while we were yet sinners, Christ died for us." Paul had no doubt that this was

the deepest meaning of the Cross.
It was the supreme proof of God's
love for sinful men.

And now we are in a position to
understand and to appreciate the
force of the argument which fol-
lows. If God has loved us, and has
given us that great proof of His
love, if when we were so sinful and
so weak, when we could do nothing
for ourselves, and had made, as
yet, no movement in the direction
of righteousness; if, then, God so
loved us, may we not confidently
reckon on His giving us all the
help we need, and doing for us all
that needs to be done in order that
we may be made perfect in holiness
and peace and joy? He who cared
enough for us to begin the good
work will surely be concerned to
complete it. If Christ loved us
enough to die for us, will not His
love avail to save us, even to the

uttermost, with that salvation
which means entire deliverance
from every evil way? "Being
reconciled through His death, shall
we not be saved by His life?"
If so great kindness was shown to
us when we were enemies, shall
we be forsaken, and left to
struggle on alone, now that we
have become friends? It is
impossible to believe it. That is
the argument.

And what is the practical bear-
ing of it all? Why just this, that
the living of that holy life, which
we find so difficult, and which is,
indeed, beyond our reach, in any
strength of our own, that the
working out of our salvation,
which seems to be a task wholly
beyond our powers, is, in truth,
God's business, which it is His
good pleasure to accomplish, that
this is His work, just as much as

that act of grace, by which we
were first quickened, and led to a
knowledge of the truth, was His
work, that we are saved, in the
fullest sense, by Christ's life, by
the "supply of His spirit," as
it is put in the Epistle to the
Philippians, by Christ's com-
munication of Himself, and not by
our own unaided efforts, though
there may be, and must be, effort
on our part, and though it must
often be laborious.

Does this seem to you to be
nothing better than a theological
subtlety?   Oh! but it is not a
theological subtlety at all.   It is
rather a fact of most practical,
most vital importance.   For, depend upon it, there is a vast
difference between the position of
the man who is painfully, and
sometimes almost hopelessly, toiling forwards in the way of holiness,

who is vainly, however nobly,
struggling to make himself good,
and the position of that man who
is a partaker of the life and
power which Christ communicates.
It is the difference between failure,
thraldom, despondency on the one
hand, and victory, freedom, joy
on the other. The man who has
been long without food may press
on for a time with his work, but
he must break down sooner or
later, and all that he does will be
done wearily and with difficulty.
But let him have such food as
suits him, and a sufficient supply,
and what a change there will be!
He will be another man, and his
work will have quite another aspect
to him, and will be done, if not
without exertion or carefulness,
which is not to be desired, at
least without any feeling of hopeless inadequacy. So let any man

be feeding daily on that Living
Bread which comes down from
heaven, and he will be "much
cheered," and will find himself
"faring bravely," and labour will
be light, and great things will
seem possible to him, which otherwise would be far out of his reach.
He will have spirit for anything.

And I think we have much to
learn, that we are but beginners in
the Divine life, if we have never
learned anything of this salvation,
which comes through the supply
of Christ's spirit. We may pass
for religious people. We may be
unhesitating believers in all the
articles of the Christian Creed.
We may be devout worshippers,
diligent workers, useful citizens,
upright, conscientious, earnest
men, and yet how little we
know of the Christian Redemption, in the fulness and the power

and the glory of it! What a dull, dead thing the most scrupulous orthodoxy may be, and how dead may be all our dead works, and how destitute of all the glow and warmth of life our worship may be, yes, and must be, if we are not sharers in that glorious power, and that clear vision of things invisible by which the world may be overcome! That is our great need. Not so much more money or better methods, or more correct opinions, but more of that life which Christ came to give us abundantly, more of that Divine Spirit Who in us will bring forth all His fruits of love and joy and peace, more of that might, in the power of which we shall be able to do all things.

And how comes this Divine life? How may we get this supernatural power? There is only one possible

answer to that question. It comes
through faith. But, again, what
is faith? There is a faith which
is nothing more than an indolent
assent of the mind, and there is
a faith which is a vague confidence
in God that, somehow, He will
take care of us and bring us at
last to perfection. But it is not
such faith which saves the soul.
The saving faith is something more
vital, more energetic. It is something which brings us face to face
with Christ, which involves a clear
apprehension, on our part, of His
character, His personality, and the
yielding of ourselves to His in-
fluences, and the deliberate and
solemn acceptance of His help,
and the consecration of our wills
to His service.

That is faith, and it must be
present in some degree if we are
to receive from Christ that which

He is prepared to give. There are certain men of whom it is said that they have a magnetic, almost a mesmeric, power over their fellows. They cast a strange spell over those who are brought under their influence. Sometimes their control over other minds is so extraordinary that there seems to be practically no limit to it. They can do what they please with their patients, if that is the right word. They govern them for the time being absolutely. These are facts which are well known to medical science, and, indeed, they are facts which have sometimes attracted a good deal of public attention. They have seemed to be so remarkable, so significant. And even when the power exerted by one mind over another is not carried to an extent so abnormal, so perilous, as we may think, yet in our ordinary

relations with each other we know
how men of character and strong
will can infect their followers with
their own spirit, can put into them
life, and energy, and hope.

But in order to get strength and
inspiration in this way from our
fellow-men it is necessary for us
to believe in them, to put ourselves
into their hands, to let them come
in and possess us, as it were, for a
while. If we are distrustful and
rebellious we shall get no help
from them. We shall be like people
who keep their doors and windows
closed so that the light and air
cannot come in.

Now I cannot but think that
there is a suggestive analogy here,
between this kind of personal influence which one man may exert
over another, and the vitalising
and inspiring grace that comes
from Jesus Christ.   Stand aloof

from Christ and He cannot help
you. Harden your heart; wrap
yourself up in your self-sufficiency
and pride; insist, in your self-
will, on maintaining your own
independence, and He will be
little or nothing to you. How is
it possible for Him to be of much
service in that case? Your guide
cannot help you up the steep
mountain path if you are afraid to
take his hand. The doctor has
not a fair chance if you will not
put yourself under his care. But
put away your pride; let yourself
go; trust yourself to Christ, as
the birds trust themselves to the
air, as the ship when it is
launched commits itself to the
buoyant waters. Fling open wide
the gate, and let that King of
Glory come in, that Lord of all
power and might, that Sun and
dear Saviour of the soul, let Him

come in, and see whether the effect
of that self-abandonment will not
be that you shall be filled with His
fulness and saved by His life. If
thus we are willing to die we shall
surely find that we are beginning
to live with that life which is life
indeed. " What multitudes," says
Dr. Sears, " have found not only
rest, but everlasting joy at the feet
of Jesus Christ, simply by giving
themselves away to Him in an unbounded trust, who never tried to
excogitate the methods of the
atonement or those eternal laws
of being which it fulfils. In
spiritual things, as in natural, the
law of supply and demand is sure
in its operations and last results.
What we want in Christ we
always find in Him. When we
want nothing we find nothing.
When we want little we find little.
When we want much we find

much. But when we want everything, and get reduced to complete
nakedness and beggary, we find
in Him God's complete treasure-
house, out of which come gold and
jewels, and garments to clothe us,
wavy in the richness and glory of
the Lord."

The Glorious Majesty of His Kingdom.

"The glorious majesty of His kingdom."
—PSALM CXLV. 12.

THERE are many prophecies and dreams in the Old Testament of a great and glorious Kingdom that was one day to be established in the earth. There was to be a golden age in the future to which the people of God looked forward wistfully, and in the thought of which they found comfort amid all their discouragements and sorrows. The great day might not come in their time. Still it would come. And they saw it in vision, and rejoiced.

Then, at length, in the fulness of time it did come. The Messiah, long expected and prayed for, appeared. "Christ," we read, "began to preach and to say, The time is fulfilled and the Kingdom of God is at hand." Here, then, it would seem, was the realisation of all those ancient hopes. At last the happy day has dawned. The golden age has begun. Here is the Kingdom with its King.

But is there any correspondence between the Kingdom which was actually founded by Christ, and the Kingdom which had been anticipated and foretold by the prophets? They had spoken in the most glowing language of its greatness and splendour. They had talked of its "glorious majesty." It was something, as they prefigured it, that was magnificent beyond description, something that would far transcend all the glories of the

4

reign of David or the Court of
Solomon, something that it would
be the highest possible privilege
to belong to. Such was their
dream. But did the dream come
true? Was the Kingdom that
was at hand when Jesus began
His ministry so fine a thing? We
know that the prevailing opinion
among the Jews was that it was
not a fine thing at all. This
Messiah was not the Messiah
they had been looking for, and
they could see nothing glorious or
majestic in the Kingdom which
was beginning to shape itself
under His teaching and guidance.
To their eyes it was a dull and
sorry affair, having small attraction for any ambitious or patriotic
soul; and its inaugurator was
altogether a disappointing Person.
When they saw Him there was no
beauty that they should desire

Him. What was it that they saw? They saw the son of a mechanic, a man of the people, simply clad, who moved among the cottages of the poor, and was even found in the houses of the publicans; who talked in the homeliest language, and seemed content to take upon Himself the humble duties of a country doctor or itinerant preacher; who had a a following of fishermen, and others in like position—men of no social importance and slender education; who made no sort of public show, who was without wealth, without arms, any of those instruments and appliances by which great movements can be carried to a successful issue.

This was what they saw; and they were very contemptuous. Was this what they had been

waiting for so long? Was it thus
that God was going to fulfil the
promises made to their fathers?
There was no greatness in this
kingdom. It was not a kingdom
worth belonging to. It was not
worth calling a kingdom. Jesus
might speak of Himself as King
of the Jews, but it was an absurd
misnomer. It was playing with
words to use such language. They
preferred Cæsar to such a King.

So it was in the early days of
the Kingdom. And in subsequent
times it has often seemed to on-
lookers that whatever might be
said in praise of the Kingdom of
Christ, and whatever attraction it
might have for a certain order of
minds, it could not honestly be
said that there was anything very
glorious about it. The Roman
Empire, with its vast wealth, its
irresistible power, its world-wide

rule, was something that did appeal to the imagination. The master of that Empire, seated on his throne, and clad in the Imperial purple, was no doubt a majestic being. To be a citizen of such an Empire was no mean honour. But in the days when the Empire was still flourishing, and the throne of the Cæsars unshaken, how pitiful, how small a thing the Christian Church appeared. "You see your calling, brethren," says St. Paul, half sadly, half proudly, "how that not many wise men after the flesh, not many mighty, not many noble, are called." Yes, it was certainly not a magnificent thing to be a Christian. That was the general feeling among polite and educated men. "These Christians," says Celsus, "are shoemakers, weavers, fullers, illiterate clowns." Another

writer describes the Christians as
being drawn from the lowest dregs
of the people, and as understand-
ing nothing of civil matters, not
to speak of things that were
divine. Even Jerome acknow-
ledges that they came not from
the Academy or the Lyceum, but
from the lowest classes. What
majesty could there be in a
Kingdom composed of such elements?

And we may be tempted to say
that it has always been so, and
that greatness and splendour have
belonged to the world, and not to
the Church, or only to the Church,
in so far as it has allied itself to
the world, and has been enriched
and adorned by it. What is the
feeling that you find prevailing in
many quarters? Is it not this,
that religious people, unless they
have a great deal beside their

religion, unless they are people
who have wealth and position, and
such opportunities as wealth and
position bring, that people who
make religion their chief concern,
are living a life which must be
a very tame and limited affair.
Oh! the dulness of the religious
life! That is what some of you
are thinking. You may allow that
it is a wise thing to become religious, and even a necessary thing,
a thing that has to be submitted to
sooner or later. But how slow,
how uninteresting a thing it is,
this religious life! It can scarcely
be called life. To be in Society,
that is life! to be mixed up with
the affairs of the city or the affairs
of the State, to have the control
of some great business, to be
thrown into contact with distinguished people, to be a soldier, to
be a conspicuous figure at the Bar,

to be a favourite actor, a popular
author, a famous singer, that is
life! The thought of such careers
is enough to stir the blood. They
are careers that are worth the
ambition of a man of spirit. But
to be just a religious man—a
Christian! Well, of course, it is
a proper and excellent thing : but
if you are going to take up the
religious life seriously, then fare-
well to all natural ambitions. The
grand thing would be to command
a military expedition, to lead your
men to victory, and to come home
and be received everywhere with
acclamations, and made a peer of
the realm. That would indeed be
a splendid thing. There is a
romance, a glamour about such an
achievement. But to spend half
one's life in some lonely part of
the mission field, or among the
poor and unhappy and sinful of

the cities and villages of our own
country, to give oneself up to the
work of teaching and comforting
and healing and saving, without
any excitements, without praise,
without even, perhaps, the grati-
tude of those whom one is trying
to help; why, there seems to be
nothing in such a career to furnish
a fit theme for a ballad, or to
suggest a decoration or a title.
To cut men down right and left,
to kill and to destroy, and to leave
the field victorious, that is worth
living for! But to be lifting up
those that are cast down and
cheering those that are desolate!
Perhaps you have never felt much
disposition to distinguish yourself
in that way. You will leave such
things to those who cannot look
for more brilliant careers.

Well, there are no doubt many
who will sympathise with you in

that way of thinking; but I am
not sure that you will not feel, if
you take the trouble to look into
the matter a little, that you are
taking rather a childish view of
things. Perhaps if we were a
little wiser we should not be so
much beguiled by the mere glitter
on the surface. We should feel
that "mere noise repels"; we
should understand that the music
hall point of view is not the most
rational point of view after all,
and that the deeds that win popular applause and bring a man's
name to the front are not, by any
means, the greatest deeds.

Should it not sober us a little,
do you not think, should it not
bring us, bewitched as we so often
are, to our senses, to remember Jesus
Christ, and His way of looking at
things, and His manner of life?
It did not appear to Him that the

Kingdom which He said was at
hand was a poor thing, a thing of
doubtful value, a thing to be
apologised for, a thing that might
be of some use and comfort to
those unfortunate and forlorn
persons who had little or no
chance in this world, but not a
thing which was worth the attention of those who had careers
before them. It was not so that
He regarded the matter. He took
quite a contrary view. To Him
all the kingdoms of the world and
all the glory of them were not to
be compared with that Kingdom,
the gates of which were now
thrown open. John the Baptist
had been a famous man. Among
them that had been born of women
there had not been a greater than
John the Baptist; but he was less
than the least of the citizens of
the Kingdom of Heaven. That

was a strong thing to say, but
Christ said it. The richest man in
the land could not do better than
sell all that he had, if by so doing
he might find his way into this
Kingdom. So Jesus thought. I
suppose, He might have been a
victorious general if he had chosen.
But he did not choose. He chose
something that He felt was greatly
to be preferred. He would deliver
not Israel only, but mankind. Do
you think that He was dazzled by
the splendour of Herod, a man
who cared much, as all the Herods
did, for display? or that He
looked with envy at Pilate, who
represented the majestic and
invincible Roman Empire, or that
He ever wished that it might be
possible for Him to sit on the
throne of Tiberius? It is a
profanity to suggest such things.
He knew secrets that were hidden

from Pilate. There was a glory
belonging to Him that transcended
beyond measure the glory of any
earthly court. He wielded a
power that would one day be
acknowledged to be unspeakably
mightier than the power that any
of the long line of Emperors could
claim. And does it not seem to
you that the thought of Jesus
Christ, and of the view of life
which He held, and the aims
which He set before Him, ought
to make us feel ashamed of our
foolish judgments and rather
paltry ambitions? Think of it.
Was it not a greater thing for
Him to be going about, as we are
told that He did, preaching the
Gospel of the Kingdom, and
healing all manner of sickness,
and all manner of disease among
the people, and talking to poor
troubled men and women about

the value of their souls and the
goodness of their Father in
Heaven, than if He had sat on the
imperial throne and lorded it over
mankind? The people wanted to
make Him a king once. There
was His opportunity if He had
cared to seize it. But would there
have been a hundredth part of the
glory about the crown which they
would have placed on His head,
that we, and all the world, can
discern in that crown of thorns
which He wore so meekly?

It is good to think of that mind
which was in Him. And good,
too, to remember how entirely His
disciples came in the end to look at
things in the Divine way. At first
they had something of the child's
view of majesty and splendour.
They thought much of thrones, and
of being clothed with authority,
and of being regarded as great

people. But all that passed away. Their eyes were opened and they awoke and understood. And they put away childish things. And Peter could see that the true glory was in following in the Master's steps; in being gentle and patient, even under oppression. And John, recalling the life which Jesus had lived when He dwelt among us, could say that he and his fellow-disciples had beheld in that Word made flesh a glory as of an Only-begotten from the Father, and could bear witness that he had seen and heard things more wonderful than all that the world could show. And Paul, who had made so much in former days of those things which had been, as he said, gain to him, those advantages of birth and station and worldly honour which are generally so dear to the human heart—

Paul could say that he counted all
these things to be loss for Christ,
in comparison with the excellency
of the knowledge of Christ, and
that there was nothing he cared to
glory in but the cross of Christ.
It had seemed a great thing to be
a Hebrew of the Hebrews. It
seemed now to be an infinitely
greater thing to be a bond-slave
of Jesus Christ. The light which
shone when the morning stars
sang together, at the creation of
the world, was but dim and transi-
ent in comparison with the light
of the knowledge of the glory of
God which had shone, in the later
days, in the face of Jesus Christ.
Remember, too, how the writer to
the Hebrews speaks to those poor,
desponding saints who were the
heirs of the ancient splendours of
Israel, and who were feeling that
they had forfeited much in becom-

ing Christians. He shows them that what they had lost was as nothing in comparison with their gains. They were immeasurably better off than any of their fathers had been, even in the most prosperous days of the undivided Kingdom. He refers to Mount Sinai; and then in a familiar passage, full of exalted feeling and holy amazement at the calling and destiny of the believer, he says, "But ye are come unto Mount Zion, and unto the city of the living God, the heavenly Jerusalem, and to an innumerable company of angels, to the general assembly and church of the First-born, which are written in Heaven, and to God, the Judge of all, and to the spirits of just men made perfect, and to Jesus, the mediator of a new Covenant, and to the blood of sprinkling that speaketh better things than that of Abel." That is what the new dispensation meant to the Apostles. It was no disappointment to them, when they came to understand it. The Kingdom had not come as they dreamt it would come, when first they heard the call of Jesus and obeyed it, and became His disciples; but it had come in a form that was to them incomparably more glorious. Those Old Testament prophets had not foreseen one-half of the glory that was to be revealed in Christ. The reality far exceeded their fairest hopes and their brightest visions. To these men, these Apostles, despised as they were, poor, persecuted, made as the filth of the world, and the offscouring of all things, it seemed such a wonderful, such a glorious thing to be a Christian.

And I am sure that if God in His mercy reveals things as they are to us, if we are so touched by His Spirit, so born from above, as to be able to see that Kingdom of which Jesus spoke, we shall feel as the Apostles felt. We shall feel that the world, with all its movement and glitter, its sensations and excitements, is an intolerably poor and dull place in comparison with the Church. That is what we shall feel if there is given to us anything like an adequate conception of what the Church really is. We shall feel, then, a great sorrow and compassion for those poor men who are spending all their strength in gathering together a little heap of gold, which must before long be scattered, and are caring for nothing else; and for those who are struggling and manœuvring to be made much of

in society and to be brought to the
front, soon to fall back into ob-
scurity; and for those unfortunate
people whose chief idea and aim
are to be comfortable, and to have
things made easy for them.   Such
notions and such ways will seem
to us to be deplorable, melancholy
in the extreme, if we have come to
know what is the hope of our
calling, and what the glory of our
inheritance, as the children of God.
Try to realise what that high
calling is.   To belong to the Kingdom means that you have been
brought into most sacred and
intimate union and fellowship with
Christ Himself.   You see Him
crowned with glory and honour,
and you know that you are called
to share in that glory and honour.
He is not your Saviour only, He is
your Leader, your Friend, your
Brother, your Companion.   Can

you conceive of any loftier privilege? Surely we can go without the camp proudly, and with uplifted heads, if we are going to join Him there. How poor every earthly distinction must appear to those who know that they have been called to His fellowship, and can say that they have obeyed the call. There is none like Him, and if we are one with Him, our cup of blessing is full. But there is more than this. For consider into what society we are called when we become Christians, and by whom we are made welcome. When we cast in our lot with Christ, we take our place with all the noble and the true-hearted of every age, with the glorious company of the Apostles, and the goodly fellowship of the prophets, and the noble army of martyrs, and the holy Church throughout all the world. Into

this great family of Heaven we
become incorporated, and we are
received with gladness, and treated
with all love and respect. Is that
something to be thought little of ?
It would be a fine thing to be
buried in Westminster Abbey, to
lie there with all the illustrious
dead of this great nation. But
how much better a thing to live in
all fulness of life, and to live for
ever in the company of those who
have been redeemed from death,
and have been made to sit in the
heavenly places with Christ Jesus.

Remember, too, the grandeur of
the work which is given us to do
as the servants and friends of
Christ. It is ours to share in the
building up of that Kingdom into
which we have been called. And
is not that an occupation worthy
of all our noblest powers ? It is
sometimes our complaint that we

are appointed to trivial tasks, and
condemned to a tedious and un-
romantic routine of labour. And,
looked at under some aspects, our
employments must often appear to
be humble and uninteresting. But
if we are at work in the Kingdom
of Christ then everything that we
do, yes, and even everything that we
suffer, has a sacred and an eternal
significance. For by all that we
are doing, and by all that we are
enduring, if we are trustful, and
patient, and loving, and holy, we
are playing our part as builders of
the New Jerusalem, the everlasting
City of God. Every deed done in
the Adorable Name, every word
spoken in obedience to the Christian Spirit, every sorrow meekly
and unselfishly borne, every gift,
every sacrifice, every honest
struggle, every pure desire, every
detail and incident of our life is a

contribution to that most glorious enterprise, the accomplishment of which is the fulfilment of the world's hope, and the satisfaction of the Redeemer's travail. What meaning there is, what worth there is in this poor human life when we consider these things! How good a thing, how sublime a thing it is to be a man, if one may also be a Christian!

Surely, when we ponder the matter, we shall see that it is not using language too strong to speak of the glorious majesty of this kingdom, which our Lord opened for us when He overcame the sharpness of death.

The Consecration of the Wise-Hearted.

"And Moses called Bezaleel and Aholiab, and every wise-hearted man in whose heart the Lord had put wisdom, even every one whose heart stirred him up, to come unto the work to do it."—EXODUS XXXVI. 2.

THE wisdom of these wise-hearted men was not what we commonly understand by spiritual discernment, but rather the wisdom which is described as skill, or genius, or artistic power. Bezaleel was one who had a gift for "devising curious works in gold and silver and brass, in cutting of stone and the carving of wood, and in all sorts of cunning work." He was, in fact, a born artist. When we speak of men as inspired of God, we are not usually thinking

of the poet, or the artist, or the
man of genius in any other direction. And yet the genius of these
two men is said to be of God. And
why not? What fine faculty is
there of hand or brain which is
not of God? What hast thou
which thou hast not received?
Poets, painters, musicians, men of
science, men of letters, statesmen,
orators, all hold their powers of
God.

> Heirs of more than royal race,
> Framed by Heaven's peculiar grace,
> God's own work on earth to do.

That is Keble's description of
such men, and you cannot better
it. It is a narrow and false view
to think that it is only the
preacher or the prophet who can
be inspired.

Now Moses seems to have had
no difficulty in securing the co-

operation of these divinely-gifted
men in the great work which he
had in hand. The people at large
gave for the construction of the
Tabernacle with wonderful hearti-
ness. They continued to pour in
their contributions till Moses was
compelled to cry, " Enough." And
the wise-hearted men were not slow
to do their part. They took of
the material that was brought
to them in such abundance, and
fashioned it with their skilful
fingers into vestments for the
priests and furniture for the
Tabernacle. This, at least, was
the case with most of them. They
were not, perhaps, all equally
zealous. It is said that every man
" whose heart stirred him up "
gave himself to the work; and the
phrase suggests that there were
some whose hearts did not stir
them up, which may well have

been the case, for it almost always happens that there are some who stand languidly by when any great work is going on, and cannot be got to share in the general enthusiasm. Still, on the whole, Moses had no reason to complain of the wise-hearted men in the congregation. Nor had Solomon any cause for complaint, in a later age, when it was not the Tabernacle in the wilderness, but the Temple at Jerusalem, that was in course of construction. Then, too, there was the same generous giving, David himself having set a magnificent example. And there was the same willingness to work. "There are workers with thee in abundance," David said, before his death, to Solomon, "all manner of cunning men, for every kind of work." And Solomon found that it was so, and he had

no difficulty in carrying out his
great design. The wealth and the
genius of the nation were laid at
his feet.

But, now, one has to say with
regret and sorrow, that in the
building of that more noble and
enduring Temple, of which the
apostles and the prophets are the
foundation, and of which Jesus
Christ Himself is the chief corner-
stone, there is not always to be
found the same alacrity and zeal
among the wise-hearted. Somehow, it must be confessed, the
clever people, the people of education and culture, the most brilliant
and capable men and women, have
too often been content to stand
aloof. It was so at the beginning. It was noticed by
Annas and Caiaphas, and their
friends in the Council at Jerusalem, that Peter and John were

unlearned and ignorant men. Well,
it was true. They were not great
scholars, or men of distinction in
any way. And yet these two were
the foremost among the followers
of Jesus. The truth was that the
people who made up society, the
learned professions, the rulers and
elders, and scribes had shown but
scant sympathy with Jesus in His
work and aims. "Has any of the
Sanhedrim believed in Him?" it
was asked. No, it did not appear
that any of the Sanhedrim had
believed in Him. At the most
there were but one or two doubtful
cases. It looked, in those early
days, as though the Kingdom of
Heaven were going to be made up
entirely of the humbler classes.
Its mysteries seemed to be hidden
from the wise and prudent. It
was not that Christ had no interest
in the more educated people, but,

for the most part, these people
took no interest, certainly no
friendly interest, in Him. Even
the publicans and harlots understood Him better, and were drawn
to Him more readily. And after
the death and resurrection of Jesus
the same condition of things pre-
vailed. There were, it is true,
some few of the wise-hearted who
consecrated themselves. St. Paul
was a conspicuous example. He
was, undoubtedly, a man of station
and eminence, and remarkable
gifts, and he threw himself into
the work with extraordinary and
unfaltering zeal. But he stood
almost alone. When he came to
Rome as a prisoner, about thirty
years after his conversion, all that
the leading Jews of the city knew
of the Christians was that they
were a "sect that was everywhere
spoken against," and they seem to

have been glad of an opportunity
of learning from one who was
evidently a man of intelligence and
learning, something about these
strange people whom they did not
themselves care to approach too
closely. Paul carried none of his
friends with him when he became
a Christian. They thought he was
demented, and they would have
pitied him, I daresay, if they had
not been so excessively annoyed.

And this is what has generally
happened. What has been the
experience of the mission-field?
Why, that it is chiefly the races
that are without civilisation and
without learning that are touched
and convinced by the teaching
of the Gospel; and among the
civilised races, that it is those who
are lowest in the social scale who
are most easily reached. It is
said that when a missionary

speaks of the love of God a
Moslem will listen with contempt,
and that his features will seem to
say, though he utters no word,
"What absurdity, what blas-
phemy, is this!" And that the
Hindoo will listen with a scep-
tical smile, as though he would
say, "Do you suppose I am going
to believe a story like that?"
But the low caste, or no caste,
man of the hill, when he hears
the message, will listen with
wonder and awe, as though he
would say, "Can it indeed be
true? Is it possible that God
can care for men like that?"

And among the people who
profess Christianity in our own
land you know that it is frequently
a cause for sorrow and disappointment that so many of those who
would seem from their education
and abilities best qualified to take

6

part in this great work of building
up the spiritual temple of God
among men, are disposed to stand
somewhat coldly aside, as though
they had no very particular concern with Christ. There have
been, of course, men like Henry
Martyn, like Heber, like Vanderkemp, like others whom we could
name, men of wide culture and
distinguished gifts, who have consecrated themselves to the work of
Christ in heathen lands. But,
comparatively speaking, how few
of the wise-hearted have turned
their thoughts seriously in this
direction ! How few have lifted
up their eyes to behold the far-
spread harvest fields ! There are
plenty to take part in the struggles
and competitions of English life at
home, plenty who are eager to
seize every opportunity of better-
ing their position in this country.

And of such ambitions I would not say a word of discouragement. But how grateful one would be for more signs of a similar eagerness to play a brave part in this not showy, certainly, and not easy, but very sacred work! You will not find difficulty in getting young men who will go at a day's notice to India, to China, to the heart of Africa, to the very ends of the earth, as soldiers, as explorers, or in the interests of science, or in the diplomatic service, or with the view of pushing their own fortune. But the service of the Kingdom of God does not seem to attract so many volunteers.

And so of the ministry at home. It has often been a matter of complaint that few of the cleverest young men at the universities are drawn into the ranks of the Christian ministry. The Bar has its attractions, so has Medicine, so has Literature, Politics, the Civil Service, and the great Schools; but the Church! No! The pulpit has not the same charm. There are explanations no doubt of this comparative dearth of aspirants, explanations which, in some cases, are creditable to those who offer them, creditable to their honesty and their humility at least. But the fact is one to be lamented, however it may be explained. One does not grudge these brilliant young men to other professions and pursuits. But when you see how things are going, do you not feel a little jealous for Christ, and a little doubtful whether that service which is His in a peculiar and pre-eminent sense, is getting a reasonable share of the devotion and energy of our young men?

And what if we should look
to our own churches and congre-
gations and ask, Who are the
men and women who are caring
most constantly and faithfully
for the more directly spiritual
work that is always needing to be
done, who are preaching to the
poor, or visiting the sick, or teaching the young, who are "labour-
ing," to use the Apostle's phrase,
"in the Lord"? The answer to
such a question would certainly
not be wholly a discouraging
answer. There have been great
lawyers who have not thought it
beneath their dignity to teach in
the Sunday-school. There have
been men of true political genius
who have thought it did not less
become them to stand at a desk,
or in a village pulpit, and tell
simple folk what they believed
and felt about Jesus Christ, than

to rise in their place in Parliament
and discuss great questions of
State. And there have been men
of eminent artistic or literary
gifts, who have not been unwilling
to step down to those low levels of
life where so much of the work of
healing and redemption has to be
carried on, and have laboured
among the poor and miserable with
as much devotedness as if they
had been painting a magnificent
picture, or writing some noble
poem. For such men, and the
work they do, may God's Name
be praised.

But are the wise-hearted doing
their fair share of this difficult and
anxious work? There are many
humble people who are wearing
themselves out in the cause of
temperance, of purity, of mercy,
of peace, of religion. Are they
being left too much to themselves

by those who have the power to
lighten the burden of the work
incalculably, if they had but the
disposition? Did you ever read
that most stirring and pathetic
appeal that was made by Albert
Dürer, the famous Nuremburg
painter, to Erasmus, who was, I
suppose, the most accomplished
student and man of letters of his
age. Dürer was profoundly in
sympathy with Luther, and the
movement towards righteousness
and spiritual religion, in which
Luther had played so prominent
and noble a part, and the report
came to him—an unfounded report,
as it happened—that Luther was
dead; and he writes that it was very
sad and heavy to him that God
allowed so much blindness and so
much false teaching, and being
overwhelmed with a sense of the
irreparable loss that the cause of

freedom and progress had sus-
tained, he prays that God would
give to the faithful all the light
and wisdom that they needed, and
would show them their true
leader; and then he turns to
Erasmus, the shrewdest and most
brilliant man in Europe, perhaps,
and cries, "O Erasmus, stand by
us!" And that is just the cry,
though it is not always so articu-
late, that is ever coming from the
anxious and too heavily-laden
toilers in the hard fields of Christian service, to whom it seems that
the clever people, the highly-
educated people, who might do so
much and give such encourage-
ment if they would stand by them,
are inclined rather to hold aloof
and to be content with nothing
more than their mild approval or
condescending criticisms. I am
not sure that it is not sometimes

the cry of fathers to their sons, sons of whom they are proud, and for the sake of whose education they have made many sacrifices, but who, when they have been able to cut some kind of figure in society, have cared little for the things for which their fathers cared so much, and which are yet the holiest things, and the highest, and the best, let the world say what it will.

But now, if there is really any such hesitation and slackness among the wise-hearted, what is there to be said in explanation of a fact so much to be lamented? Shall we explain their slowness by saying that there are prizes to be won in the world by these brilliant people such as can scarcely be looked for in the direct service of Christ? That, no doubt, is a fact. And if we do not possess the

great gifts we admire in others,
we may fitly ask ourselves
whether, if we had their chances,
we should not be as anxious as
they are to make the most of
them? There is so much that is
possible to a really brilliant man.
It would not have been an easy
thing for Erasmus, who could hold
his own in any University or
Court in Europe, to accept all
those hard conditions, which
Dürer frankly acknowledged he
would have had to accept if he
had stood boldly with the Re-
formers. If he did that, he might
"share the fate of his Master
Christ. He might suffer shame,
and die a martyr's death." There
would have been much to give up.
There always will be. You must
remember that. And you cannot
wonder if some who have all the
kingdoms of the world, with the

glory of them brought within their
reach, should hesitate before com-
mitting themselves to a cause,
their fidelity to which is sure to
involve them in suffering and loss;
and, perhaps, we cannot wonder,
human nature being what it is,
if men will sometimes not mind
losing their own souls if they can
gain the world. Often the world
is so terribly fair and alluring, and
things unseen seem to be so far
away, and unsubstantial.

But some will say that it is not
any vulgar prize that attracts
them, but the pursuit itself—the
study, the art, for which they seem
to have been endowed with special
aptitudes. They must give their
whole strength to their profession,
if they are to do justice to it and
to themselves, and they cannot do
the one thing for which they are
fitted, in the highest possible way,

if they are to be throwing themselves into works of philanthropy
and religion. Well, if you can
say that quite honestly, if there is
really no time at all, and no grain
of energy remaining, for the things
which are Christ's, in the most
direct sense—then I would say,
Take care that you serve the
Church, and serve humanity, and
serve God in, and through, those
pursuits for which you have been
Divinely qualified, and to which
you are Divinely called. There
have been men of genius—
painters, musicians, poets, authors
—who have not been concerned to
do that, who never seem to have
been anxious to utter one word, or
to do one single thing, by which
the race of men could be helped in
their progress onwards and up-
wards. God has not been in all
their thoughts, nor man either.

And there have been those, on the other hand, whose work throughout has been so conceived and so accomplished that it has been a message and an inspiration to mankind. Four times Albert Dürer gave himself to the task of bringing home to the people of Germany the facts and realities of the life and death of the Saviour, and he was, in his way, as great a preacher of the Gospel as Luther himself. And you know how nobly some of the great painters of our own time have consecrated their genius in the same spirit. There are sermons on the walls of the new Art Gallery at Battersea which have as much power to move the imagination and rouse the conscience as any that are preached at Westminster or St. Paul's. Was Tennyson less an artist because of the moral pur-

pose that ran through all his
work? It is the fashion in some
quarters to say that art has
nothing to do with morality.
That is what is said, and, unless
you have a very narrow conception
of what morality is, it is one of
the Devil's own lies. O you, if
you are wise-hearted, if you have
clear heads and cunning fingers,
understand that according to your
gifts is the responsibility laid upon
you to use those gifts for the
Divinest ends, and be sure that
there is no happiness that endures,
and no peace that is worth possess-
ing, for those who will not bear
the yoke of Christ and put the
Kingdom and righteousness of
God above all other considera-
tions. No doubt Christ and
Christ's work do demand of us
sacrifices; but sacrifice is inevit-
able if anything is to be done in

this world that is worth doing.
And if you are prepared to spend
your strength in doing that
which is not worth doing, then
there is no one who is making
such a sacrifice as you are
willing to make. It is not
a question of sacrifice or no sacrifice. The question rather is of
the comparative value of those
things for which the sacrifices are
made. The undergraduate knows
that if his university career and
his prospects in life are to be con-
sidered he must deny himself to
some extent. He cannot give
himself up wholly to amusements,
though that may be the course
which comes to him most easily
and most naturally. He will
sacrifice those amusements rather
than abandon the purpose for
which he has come to the university, and lose the great oppor-

tunity of those golden years. And
so it is with life as a whole. You
will have to make sacrifices if you
determine to devote your life to
the highest ends. Of course you
will. There is no doubt about
that. But that which you will
sacrifice in this case will be nothing,
and less than nothing, in comparison with that which you will
have to sacrifice if you devote your
life to any lower ends. That would
be the worst conceivable kind of
waste. It would, indeed, be a
mad throwing away of your life.
It is you who are the chief loser in
the end, if you will not deny yourself and go after Christ. I spoke
of Vanderkemp. Vanderkemp was
one of the distinguished pioneers
of the London Missionary
Society, a man of sound learning and many accomplishments,
who went to live and labour and

die among the Kaffirs. When
Henry Martyn was on his way to
India the ship in which he was
sailing called at the Cape, and he
had an opportunity of meeting
Vanderkemp. There he was, with
his poor black, illiterate people
about him. " Have you ever re-
pented of your determination to
spend your days here?" said
Martyn. " I would not exchange
my work for a kingdom," was the
reply. We talk of sacrifices, but
is it not the man who is willing to
lose his life for Christ's sake and
the Gospel's who is making the
greatest sacrifices. There is no
man who wins so rich a prize as he.
There is no man who is so practical, so prudent, and so wise, no man
who makes of his life so perfect, so
glorious a success. When Francis
of Assisi had made his great re-
nunciation " he went wandering,"

Mrs. Jameson tells us, " over those beautiful Umbrian mountains from Assisi to Gubbio, singing with a loud voice and praising God for all things—for the sun which shone above, for the day and for the night, for his mother, the earth, and for his sister, the moon, for the winds which blew in his face, for the pure, precious water, and for the jocund fire, for the flowers under his feet, and for the stars above his head, saluting and blessing all creatures, whether animate or inanimate, as his brethren and sisters in the Lord." Thus it ever is, that when men are willing to have nothing they find themselves the possessors of all things. The world, which had wrecked them when they sought it, and cursed them when they clung to it, followed them with benedictions when they gave them-

selves up, with their whole heart,
to the Kingdom of God, and laid
its choicest treasures at their feet,
and soothed them with a hundred
tender ministrations. Common
things then grew sacred to them.
The winds whispered to them of
the mercies of God. The blue sky
became His sapphire throne. The
summer was His and the winter.
The trees were the trees of the
Lord. The birds sang of Him.
His lovingness breathed in the
fragrance of the flowers. He was
everywhere and they were His,
and the Almighty was their gold,
and the unsearchable riches of
Christ abounded towards them
without measure until the bliss
and the glory of it became more
than they could bear.

The Peace of Heaven.

" To be spiritually minded is peace."
—ROMANS VIII. 6.

HEAVEN is often thought of and
anticipated as a place of endless
and perfect peace, a home for
the saints, in which they may
rest from all toil and trouble
for evermore. When once they
find themselves within the gates of
the new Jerusalem they will know
that their pilgrimage, with all its
weariness and painfulness, its
sorrows and discouragements, is
come by God's mercy to an end.
There will be no more burdens to
carry or battles to fight. There
will be no more confusion or strife,
or anxieties, or oppressions, or
alarms. At last, after all the fever

and turmoil of this troubled life
upon the earth, they will be at
peace.

Such are the aspirations and
hopes which find expression in
many of our popular hymns about
the future life, and they are not
out of accord with what may be
taken to be the prevailing conception of Heaven, a conception to
which we have possibly assented
without demur.

But it may be worth our while
to ask ourselves what it is that we
really mean. That there is truth
in the doctrine implied in thése
hymns we may acknowledge at
once. There must be peace in
Heaven if it is to be Heaven at
all. The instinct of the Christian
heart is not likely to have been
altogether at fault. But what
will be the nature and quality of
this peace which we are antici-

pating ? What will be the sources
of it ? What is the peace of
Heaven ?

An answer is possible to that
question which may seem at first
to be a very true and proper
answer, but which on reflection
will scarcely satisfy us. Why
shall we be at peace in Heaven ?
Because there, it may be said,
there will be none of those things
which try us and distract us here.
Our work will be done ; our
fighting will be over. We shall
be like the labourer, who
puts away his implements at
close of day, like the soldier who
hangs up his shield and sword,
and takes his rest after the long
campaign.

That has a pleasant sound. And
yet consider ! Is it truly a prospect that has so great a charm for
you ? It is taken for granted that

repose and tranquillity are what
everybody in his heart desires.
But is it so in fact? Of course,
there are times when we are in ill-
health, or have unusual difficulties
to contend with, or have been
harassed with one thing or
another, when we do feel inclined
to say with the Psalmist, "O that
I had wings like a dove, then
would I fly away and be at rest."
But is that your habitual feeling?
Is it the prevailing spirit among
those who are doing Christ's work
in the world to-day? I cannot
believe it. I have known Christian people who have been compelled, through force of circumstances, to give up their work for
a time to whom that period of
inactivity has been a heavy trial to
patience. They have longed to be
at work again. It has been quiet
enough where they have been. No

harsh and jarring sounds have
been allowed to vex the tranquillity
of their sick chamber. Not any
of those sights, which are so often
to be seen in squalid homes and
crowded streets, have been visible
there. Fresh flowers have been
brought to them by loving friends.
They have received nothing but
kind words and the most gentle
treatment. And they have had
little or no pain or discomfort.
And yet it was not long before
they became impatient, or as
impatient as it seemed to them
lawful to be. They were eager to
get back to the courts, and alleys,
and miserable homes, and helpless,
hopeless, struggling, sinful men
and women. It was not that the
work which they had been doing
had not been hard. It had been
very hard. They had broken down
under the terrible strain of it. It

was not that it had been free from
sorrows and disappointments.
There had been these in abundance. But for all that they loved
their work. Their heart was in it.
Their treasure was there among
those unhappy, much - needing
strugglers against destiny, whom
they were not ashamed to call
their brethren. These poor people
were their flock and they loved
them, and had no greater joy than
in the knowledge that they were
able to be of some use and comfort
to them. Do you not understand
that feeling? Have you never
shared in it? Do you really wish
for a world in which there will be
nothing to try your patience, no
difficulties to overcome, no sacrifices to be made? Many there
are, at least, I am sure who have
strength and vigour and great
compassion of heart to whom

there is attraction in hard work,
and even in hard fighting, in a
good cause, and for whom the
peaceful bowers of Paradise would
have little fascination. And it is
an unfortunate thing that Heaven
should be so conceived of as to
present little charm to those who
are not feeling tired and over-
burdened. I suppose it is because
these have been the people whose
thoughts have most naturally
turned towards to the future that
this aspect of the Heavenly state
has become so prominent. The
strong and the active, with high
courage and energy to spare, have
been engrossed with the present,
with all its interests and demands,
and those who have thought about
Heaven have been the weary and
heavy-laden, and needing rest
they have pictured Heaven to
themselves naturally as a place of

rest. But we want a Heaven
which we can all look forward
to, the thought of which will
be a joy and an inspiration to
us when we are full of strength,
and hope, and confidence, and
are glorying in the work which
God has given us to do, and
not such a Heaven as can only
have attraction for us when we
are broken down and needing
comfort and repose, being worn
out as men are worn out after the
strain of a long day's work. We
want a Heaven that our children,
our boys and girls, our high-
spirited young men and women,
can anticipate with pleasure, not
simply a haven of refuge for
the feeble and old. "We shall
have eternity to rest in," some-
body has said. But think of
resting all through eternity. Could
any prospect be less alluring?

Rest is sweet, very sweet, and welcome for a time, when we are needing it. But to be always resting! Think of men whom you have known—busy, eager, untiring in labours of love—never happy but when they were helping on some noble cause, think of them as being destined to everlasting idleness. You cannot bear to think of it. You cannot believe that all opportunity is gone from them now, and gone for ever, for the exercise of those qualities for which you honoured and loved them so much. No! if there is peace in Heaven, as there surely will be, it cannot be the peace of stagnation.

What, then, will it be like? There are certain elements in it of which I think we can speak with some confidence.

First, we may be sure that it will be the peace that comes of

love, of love to God and man, free
and abounding. What has peace
to do with love, do you ask?
Surely a great deal to do with it.
For why are men so often not at
rest within? Why do so many
things trouble them and vex them?
Why is there so much distraction
of mind, so much bitterness of
heart? Most certainly it is, in no
small measure, because their love
is so limited. There is no full
stream that flows out from them
towards all around them. That
explains their unrest. It is the
man who loves without stint who
has learned the secret of the deepest peace. God gave us hearts
that we might love with them.
That is the use of a heart; and if
we do not use our hearts as God
intended they should be used, if we
are locking-up our affections, if we
are holding back our sympathies

and giving them no outlet, no wonder there is fretfulness, and discontent, and the uneasy sense of something lacking. What else can be looked for? Thwart any deep instinct of the soul, and there will be the pain of an unsatisfied hunger, though you may not suspect the source of the trouble. To be spiritually minded is peace, and to be spiritually minded is to pour out one's soul in love. And they are in peace in Heaven, as we may believe, because they love so fully and so freely, and in such large ways, because the life of the soul which is, in its deepest essence, love, is no more fettered and confined, but has unbounded play and scope.

Again, the peace of Heaven is the peace of perfect trust. Our want of peace here is very often just want of confidence. You are

not at ease in your mind, because
you are not sure of those on whom
some interests that are dear to you
depend. You are not sure of yourself. Great responsibilities are
entrusted to your wisdom and
skill; but you are not sure whether
you are wise enough, or clever
enough, to carry the business
committed to you to a successful
issue. Or you are not sure of
some other persons who have under
their control things that are of
great value in your eyes. You are
not sure of the captain of the ship
in which you are sailing, or of
the lawyer who is conducting your
case, or of the doctor under whose
charge you have placed yourself.
Or you are not sure of God, and
of His wise and righteous govern-
ment of the world. And the con-
sequence is that you are nervous
and restless. Everything would

be different if you were more
trustful. You may be dwelling
in the midst of noise, and strife,
and confusion, and yet you will
not be disturbed or anxious if you
believe in those who are at the
helm, any more than you would be
anxious, amid all the racket and
disorder incident to the building
of a great house, if you had reason
to trust the architect and con-
tractor. To have peace you must
have faith. Was not this the
peace of Jesus? The hearts of the
disciples were failing them for fear
because of the terrible things that
seemed to be coming to pass. But
He was calm, and why? Because
He believed in His Father, and
because He was able to commit
His work and Himself to His
Father's hands. He was sure that
all would be well in the end, however dark the present might be,

and whatever wrongs He might be
called to endure from those He
loved and longed to save. And
may we not believe that our peace
in Heaven will be like His, the
peace which comes through perfect trust in the wisdom and love
of God.

But here the question may be
asked whether there will be any
need of faith and trust hereafter.
Will not all things become clear
and plain to us then? Will not
faith be swallowed up in sight?
I do not think we are at liberty to
take that for granted. We may,
indeed, be assured that many
things that are dark and mys-
terious to us now will then be
made clear. We shall know and
see much that we can only dream
of here, so that in certain ways
there will be no more demands on
our faith. But surely there is

nothing in the New Testament to
lead us to think that when the
heavenly life is entered upon we
shall be made omniscient, and
shall behold at once, and fully,
and understand, all the glory of
the universe, and shall be able to
look on to all that lies before us in
the boundless future. Could we
desire that, even if we could conceive it possible? Would it not
be a terrible thing for beings such
as we are to have everything that
is to happen through Eternity
spread out before our gaze? That
would be more than we could bear,
and we do not anticipate it. But
this we do anticipate, that we
shall then be quite sure of God,
and shall perfectly trust in His
Fatherly goodness. We shall have
no doubt that, through all ages, all
will be well, and in that simple
confidence of the child who is at

home in his Father's House, will
be our peace.

Once more, the peace of Heaven
will be the peace of those who are
fully occupied. There are other
powers belonging to us beside the
powers by which we love and
trust; and our unrest in this world
is due, in part, to the fact that
these powers are not employed or
only imperfectly employed. It is
not our labours but our limitations
which keep us in a state of dis-
quietude. There is never such a
sensation of perfect bodily content-
ment as when all the powers of the
body are in full play, and yet
not painfully fatigued or over-
strained. And there is never such
perfect spiritual rest, as when all
the powers of the spirit have been
brought fully into operation, and
a man is, so to speak, carried
wholly out of himself, and every

part of him is engaged in the work
for which it is fitted, and for which
it was created. That is the rest of
Heaven. There, they serve Him
night and day. There, room is
found, and opportunity for every
man, and not only for every man,
but for every gift and power
with which every man has been
endowed.

Is it going beyond any revelation that we have received to say
so much as this? I do not think
so. When we begin to describe,
or to imagine to ourselves, the particular occupations of Heaven, we
very quickly feel that we are
getting out of our depth. And
men of sober views are apt to turn
away with distaste from such over-
bold speculations. But we are
surely not over-bold in believing
that love in Heaven will be like
a full tide, and that trust in the

Eternal Father will never waver,
and that all the noblest powers of
the redeemed will be brought fully
into use. Nor can we be wrong
in supposing that where these conditions are fulfilled there will be
found the truest and holiest peace.
And should not that Divinest
peace be possible in a measure
here? Do you not think we
may be making a mistake in looking forward to some changed
circumstances, some other kind of
world, in which such peace and
rest will be possible, as are hopelessly beyond our reach so long as
we remain in this earthly realm of
toil and strife? Are we sure that
our longing for peace, or for such
peace as we are thinking of, is
quite worthy of Christian discipleship? Is it really a spiritual longing? We think that we are
spiritually inclined because we are

wanting to be in Heaven. But
much depends on the nature of
the Heaven in which we want
to be. Am I spiritually minded
because I am longing for ease and
pleasure ? Am I spiritual because
I desire to enjoy, in the next
world, that which I should be
ashamed to desire so earnestly in
this world ? Ought we not to
remember that the thing to be
desired is not, so much, peace,
which in itself is not a thing of
any moral value, as that spirit of
love, of faith, of consecration,
which, when it is planted within
us, brings forth peace as its necessary fruit ? We have often talked
as though we thought it was the
time, or the place, which were the
making of Heaven, whereas it is
rather the spirit, the character.
The Son of Man is in Heaven,
even in the midst of this world of

sin and trouble, because He loves
so perfectly, and trusts so entirely,
and lives only to do His Father's
will. And we are in Heaven if we
are made partakers of the spirit
of Jesus. A great future is before
us, as we hope, and it is lawful to
look forward to it with solemn
delight. But the glory of the
future may also be in great
measure the glory of the present.
We hope to go to Heaven when
we die, but there can be but
slender foundation for such a hope
unless the spirit of Heaven has
passed into us, and has possessed
us, and is ruling us now, while we
live. Your life is hid with Christ
in God. It may be so, if it is not
so in fact. And if it is so in fact,
then it means, it must mean,
peace, profound, sacred, enduring,
unutterable peace.

LONDON:

W. SPEAIGHT AND SONS, PRINTERS

FETTER LANE.